WE CAN! I know. That's wh[...]
To teach the HOW and [...]

What IS is NOW; What's YET your DREAM,
What ISN'T is all the SKY!

LOVE WHAT IS and THANK THE REST,
Then IMAGINE your TRUE DREAM!

BE THANKFUL for the MIRACLE,
As YOU stand there in-between!

"I AM AWESOME! I CAN DO THIS!"
The words to start your show...

THIS is how YOU CAN and WILL,
The things that you must know!

What MIRACLE, you ask?
Well, this is what I'm saying...

THE WORLD RESPONDS TO WHAT YOU ASK!
Just take the steps I'm laying!

For EVERYTHING IS CONSCIOUSNESS!
SEEK and YOU WILL FIND!

Walk around in the CREATION,
And be thankful for your time!

My HOPE is that you'll understand
The things that I have taught.

And pass it on for PEACE ON EARTH,
So my goal is not for naught!

Matt Scott
Author of the "Find Something Awesome!" Book Series.
www.FindSomethingAwesome.com

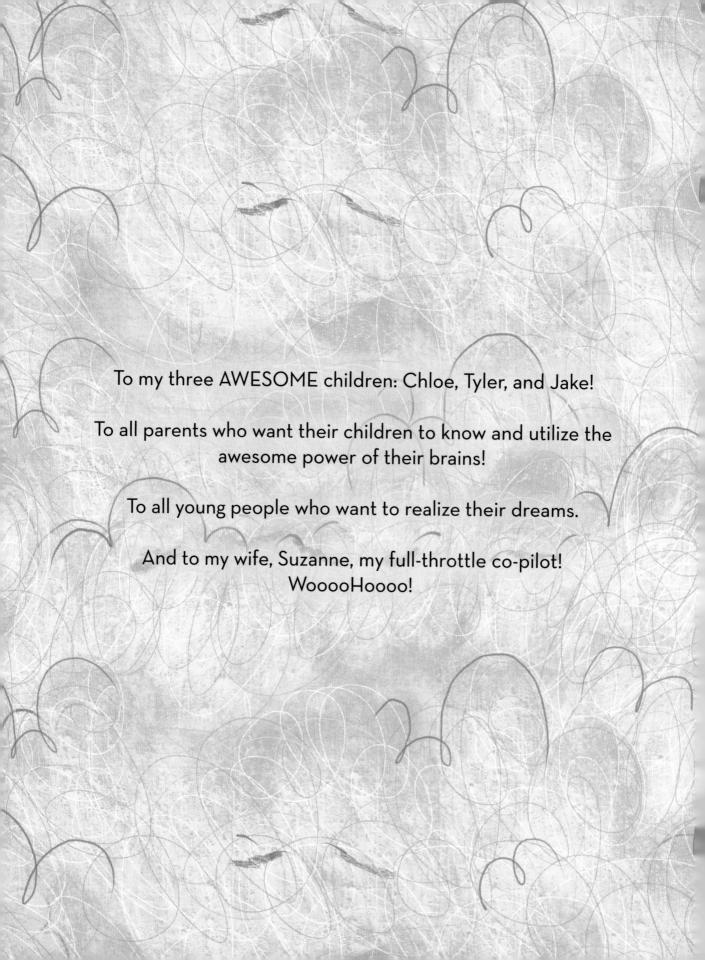

To my three AWESOME children: Chloe, Tyler, and Jake!

To all parents who want their children to know and utilize the awesome power of their brains!

To all young people who want to realize their dreams.

And to my wife, Suzanne, my full-throttle co-pilot!
WooooHoooo!

How to Use this Book

Find Something Awesome!

I AM AND I CAN!

MIND (BOX!)

A BOOK SERIES

Helping Kids Realize the Power of their Brains to Be Happy and Successful!

Level 5
Where Do You Want to Go?

A fun and friendly guide teaching kids how to properly fuel themselves to imagine and achieve their goals.

An effective parenting tool, the FIND SOMETHING AWESOME! book series introduces kids to the powers (and fun!) of Positive Thinking, Gratitude, Mindfulness, and Focused Imagination. They will learn their own Awesome Brain Power to Be Happy and Successful!

Organized into five levels, each book stands alone and also builds on the concepts introduced in earlier levels.

Read the books together with your children, then discuss the concepts each level introduces using the Questions, Awesome Brain Capabilities, and Steps as a guide.

Happiness and Success start with FIND SOMETHING AWESOME!

www.mascotbooks.com

Where Do You Want to Go?

For more information, please contact:
Mascot Books
620 Herndon Parkway #320
Herndon, VA 20170
info@mascotbooks.com

Library of Congress Control Number: 2017959032

CPSIA Code: PRT0218A
ISBN: 978-1-68401-484-2

Printed in the United States

Find Something Awesome!

I AM AND I CAN!

MIND (BOX!)

A BOOK SERIES

Helping Kids Realize the Power of their Brains to Be Happy and Successful!

Level 5

Where Do YOU Want to Go?

by **Matt Scott**

art by **Ana Sebastian**

FOLLOW YOUR HEART, BE YOURSELF

1.)

2.)

3.)

"FOLLOW YOUR HEART, BE YOURSELF,"
Advice we've all heard.

But what are the steps?
First, second, and third?

The advice is spot on,
But what are the means?

Hello
my name is

How do you do it?
Conflicting, it seems...

Some say they'll be happy
But not 'TIL they get.

This is backwards, you see.
Read this and get set!

YOU

START

This book will explain
The advice you just read

To get your TRUE GOAL,
Just like it's been said.

Where do you want to go?
What do you want to see?

IT FIRST STARTS WITH **YOU**
In order to BE!

HALF of what's needed
To witness your find,

Is literally the IMAGE
YOU make in YOUR mind!

Like pollen from a plant,
It's designed to fly out

To meet up with the world
And create a new sprout!

MIND

But yours, like a rocket ship
Inside your head,

Is half of the seed
For YOUR DREAM to be spread!

So imagine your TRUE GOAL
In full detail and size,

A picture as SEEN,
Like using your eyes.

This image, half the seed,
Your "pollen" for flight,

Is vibrating on a launch pad,
To TAKE OFF with great might!

THE IMAGE OF MY GOAL

But it still needs a fuel tank
And two things for the fuel!

These three things are a must
For a launch as a rule.

Thoughts create your feelings and
Thoughts create things!

BELIEF is the tank
All ready to fill,

Hooked up to your image
To empower this WILL!

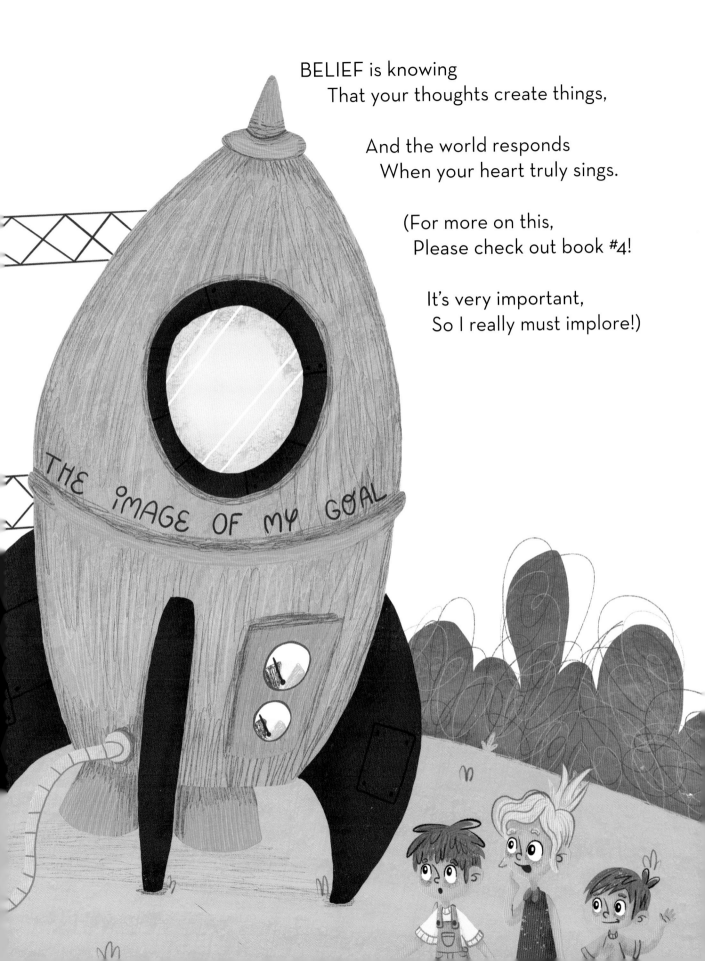

BELIEF is knowing
   That your thoughts create things,

   And the world responds
      When your heart truly sings.

      (For more on this,
         Please check out book #4!

         It's very important,
            So I really must implore!)

THE IMAGE OF MY GOAL

To fuel the tank up
There's two things to do.

One is to PRAISE
This image in you.

Praise this image
Is the same way to say:

Love your **SELF**,
this true goal in play.

This praise builds up PASSION
For your goal to succeed!

Half of the fuel,
For half of the seed.

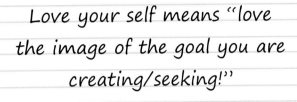

Love your self means "love
the image of the goal you are
creating/seeking!"

The second thing to do
To fuel this conceive,

Is be THANKFUL for the image
You're ABOUT to receive!

Thankfulness from FAITH:
"IT WILL!" not "IT MIGHT."

Like being thankful a rock falls
When dropped from a height.

This PRAISE and THANKS
To the image you paid

Is now a fueled-up half seed
For your DREAM to be MADE!

"For every action, there is an equal and opposite reaction."

Translation: Give love, Get love. So love anything or everything. Love your family, love your home, love the blue sky, love the sun, love a tree, love the air, love your shoes, it doesn't matter what it is, it HAS TO Give Back!

Be sure that you never
Run out of this fuel.

There's a TRUE way to source it
And it's totally cool:

FIND SOMETHING AWESOME
Where you currently are!

PRAISE and be THANKFUL
For what's come so far!

This action's called LOVING,
It's GIVING from YOU!

**This is the FIRST thing
That YOU have to DO,**

'Cuz when you are GIVING,
The WORLD gives it BACK!

(Proven by Newton
With science now fact!)

This love that's **RETURNED**
Is what you now use...

(Started from YOU,
No thing you can lose!)

This source's RETURN
Brings **HAPPY** to feel,

Like thanking a rainbow,
TRUE fuel when it's real.

This **OPENS YOUR MIND**,
The place **YOU** create,

And is used as the TRUE source
For the two actions to take.

AKA IMAGINATION
AKA MIND
AKA SELF

The action of Finding Something
Awesome and being thankful is
called LOVING. The action of loving
OPENS YOUR MIND!

To prove that this works:
Something beautiful **UN**-seen

Cannot make you happy
Until you FIRST see it gleam.

YOU praise it, be thankful,
And THEN in return,

It GIVES BACK this good feeling,
True fuel to RE-BURN!

It's ENDLESS this source,
It never runs out!

And it all STARTS from YOU!
To this there's no doubt!

Have you ever been angry or sad, and
not aware of a beautiful sunset, then
looked up and saw it and felt happiness?
YOU started and did it, not the sunset.
The beautiful sunset doesn't have
effective power until you FIRST tell it
it's beautiful!

Be careful,
You'll be TEMPTED to use
Other sources than this,

But THIS fuel is FAKE,
And runs out quite quick!

You'll know this has happened
By how you may ACT,

To DEFEND this false source
And take you OFF-TRACK!

Maybe a bad feeling?
Your stomach in knots?

Please remember that FEELINGS
Come from your THOUGHTS!

MIND

Track a bad feeling back to the thought that
created it... the original thought will always
source from what you thought someone ELSE
or some THING was thinking... Using it as a
source for your confidence... YOU can Love
YOU, so you don't have to do this!

So **PAY ATTENTION to your FEELINGS,**
And WHY you're enforcing.

These things below
Are a list of bad sourcing:

SLOTH to conserve
When it can't ever empty.

LUST to assure
More is not plenty.

ENVY to want
A thing you can get.

ANGER when challenged
What's never a threat.

GLUTTONY and GREED
'Cuz it's never enough

When you use this false fuel
To fill your tank up.

And the sneakiest of all
Is energy from PRIDE.

Confidence as frail
As a canyon is wide.

Pay attention to this
'Cuz **YOU** are not these desires!

Let them go past **YOU**
Then raise your chin higher!

Let these desires go past you!

Example? You have ONE cookie, but you are sad because you want TWO. The greed desiring TWO cookies ruins the good feeling of having ONE! Let the desire to have two cookies go past YOU and be thankful for the awesome cookie you have! Coming back to your NEW NOW!

Temptations these are!
Your biology's cane.

Your BODY'S desire
Hardwired in your brain.

And deadly they are
To your dream you will find.

'Cuz where they really came,
IS FROM YOUR SHUT MIND!

Some people call this the "monkey brain!" We all have it... Don't let it lead your life's decisions or actions!

FAKE FUEL - NO TRESPASSING // FAKE FU

WHAT
ARE YOU
THINKING
'CUZ MY
MIND IS NOT!

Once tapped into THESE sources,
FEAR can arise...

'Cuz your brain knows if lost,
Its FUEL SOURCE JUST DIES!

So recognize these feelings
And know WHY they came:

YOU were looking FOR fuel
To boost up your game!

YOUR MIND turned right **off**,
Your confidence a mess!

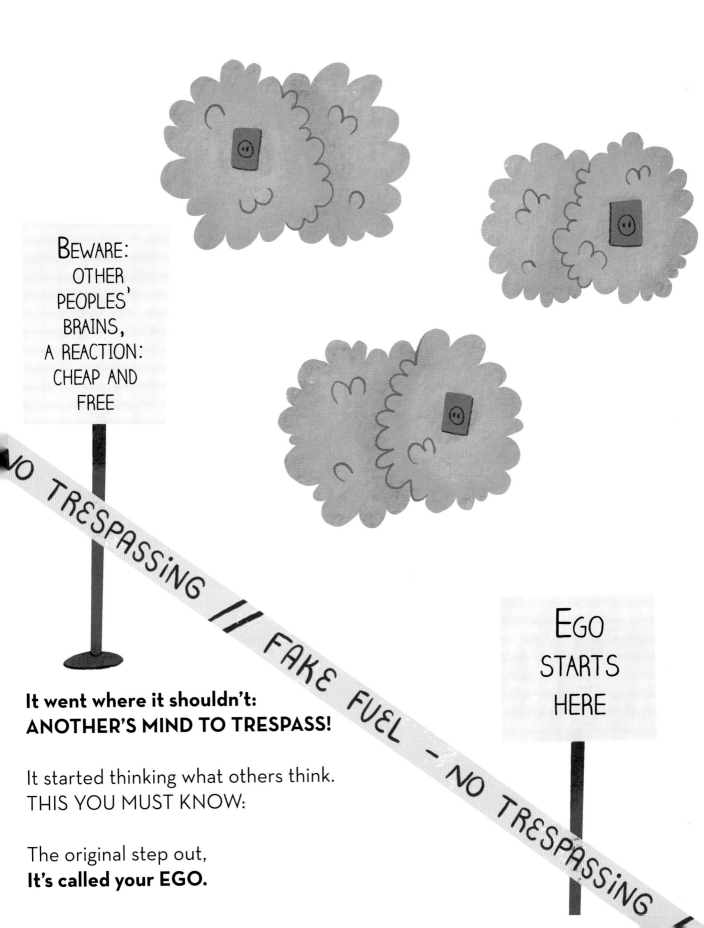

BEWARE:
OTHER
PEOPLES'
BRAINS,
A REACTION:
CHEAP AND
FREE

NO TRESPASSING // FAKE FUEL - NO TRESPASSING

EGO
STARTS
HERE

It went where it shouldn't:
ANOTHER'S MIND TO TRESPASS!

It started thinking what others think.
THIS YOU MUST KNOW:

The original step out,
It's called your EGO.

Your brain now NEEDS SOMEONE
To keep itself strong,

But INSECURITY this is,
'Cuz the fuel source is wrong.

Pay attention to this
'Cuz it's easy to do.

A reaction indeed
To a challenging cue.

(When does it do this,
You ask with a turn?

Check out book #3!
From there you will learn.)

Your ego tries
To TAKE fuel WITHOUT giving.

It turns into failure
And keeps dreams from living.

Your ego seeks OTHERS
To GIVE you this fuel,

**When YOU GIVING FIRST
Is the task for renewal!**

Thinking what others think
Then allows the situation

Of REACTING to OTHERS'
Negative vibration!

This insecurity is MINDLESS
Like a boat you can't steer.

Anxiety and panic,
Feeling helpless, OH DEAR!

When YOUR mind is closed
Your brain makes you BLAME...

...Feeling judged or frustrated?
From here's where it came.

Your brain is trespassing,
Going where it should NOT.

**Use your OWN MIND
To create your OWN thought!**

Be sure you're not wanting a thing
So others will like you.

Liking you is YOUR job,
THEN they will too!

TRIGGER

FIND SOMETHING
AWESOME!

Some people actually LOOK
for problems so they can use it
as a trigger reminder to Find
Something Awesome and Create
a new solution!

Negative thinking ALL of this is.
Your SELF it's sure NOT!

When you're seeking this fuel,
It happens on the spot!

When you feel the negative,
Like "not good enough,"

Feelings to quit,
Or ANY bad stuff...

Know this was your EGO
From the source you've plugged in,

AND YOU CAN MAKE IT ALL STOP
WITH TWO STEPS TO BEGIN!

STEP 1:
USE these bad feelings
For what's called a "trigger."

Think, "It's time to refuel
From something much bigger!"

STEP 2:
Re-FIND SOMETHING AWESOME!
And thank the sky just above!

And know this is how
You start things with LOVE!

Now take a deep breath
And smile as you go.

This day was made
FOR YOU as you know!

Get this energy back, LOVE YOU!
And start over again.

Refuel your image
And stick to your PLAN...

So it can meet with the sky
And make something great!

Like HALF of a seed,
A male to its mate!

The mate in this case,
The OTHER HALF of the seed...

Is the UNIVERSE itself
AROUND what you see!

Know this day was made for YOU.

Rejoice and be glad in it.

Think of everything you see as a giant TV screen... the real workings are behind the screen bringing you the image.

Biology can explain,
'Cuz YOU KNOW that it takes

Both a FATHER and a MOTHER,
For the baby it makes!

Your IMAGINATION IS the father,
The Universe, the mother.

Your DREAM is made
From them joining together!

Your idea, half a seed
To the mother and her womb,

Comes to LIGHT as you sought
Like a door off a tomb...

DIRECTOR

DIRECTOR

DIRECTOR

Now playing:

"The Image you made of your goal!"

Be sure to picture what your goal looks like in your imagination... otherwise, how will the universe know how to respond? And how would you know when you've accomplished something you've sought or not?.

...STARTED with LOVE from YOUR giving,
Returned and UN-ENDED,

With GOOD FEELINGS to fuel YOU
AND your image intended!

But please, LOVE WITHOUT WANTING
Any love in return,

'Cuz only IN GIVING you get,
As physics did learn!

When you love without want,
You TRULY receive!

An OPEN HEART this is called,
And will fill your believe!

An open heart is loving without wanting in return! Practice complimenting someone so they feel good... and watch how that makes YOU feel!

A loving/giving PURPOSE unlocks the path of your TRUE POTENTIAL to find your dream! Love YOU so you are not NEEDING it from others!

- LOVE YOUR WORLD AND BE THANKFUL
- LOVE YOU
- LOVE THE IMAGE OF YOUR GOAL!

Your SELF is the IMAGE you created in Your IMAGINATION. This "SELF," Your MIND, and Your IMAGINATION are all the same exact thing!

So, STEP 1 is LOVING
The WORLD that you see,

Thanking the SKY, then
step 2 and step 3!

STEP 2:
Now love YOU right now!
"I am awesome!" you say!

STEP 3:
Then love the image
You are seeking this day!

Following your heart
Means love and then go

To the pathway that opens
From doing just so.

And the pathway that opens
Is the one that you sought,

To the image YOU made
From your SELF that YOU thought!

Now do you understand
The advice from the start?

TO TRULY BE YOUR SELF
YOU MUST FOLLOW YOUR HEART!

From loving what IS
To loving what's sought!

BEING THANKFUL FOR BOTH,
The most powerful thought!

Thanking the Universe
Then thanking YOU CAN...

...With this gift you've been given
To achieve your true plan!

A circular path
Of renewing now flows.

Smile and BREATHE
As AWARENESS now grows!

YOUR IMAGINATION

1) Love What IS (the material world you see),

2) Thank WHAT ISN'T, (the sky/universe around what you see),

3) Praise WHAT ISN'T YET! (The image you seek in your imagination).

Witness your world,
Picture your dream,

Love unconditionally,
And **STAND IN BETWEEN.**

This place that you stand is
"RIGHT NOW," your tarmac!

The world in FRONT of you
Your idea in the BACK.

This "NOW" is YOU!
Stand up and take aim!

Open your eyes
And witness the game...

3... 2... 1...
Get ready to go!

The ignition switch,
Just the words down below:

"I am awesome, I can do this,"
Please say in your head!

Be thankful for this miracle
Like it's been said!

Your rocket takes off
With your action to find,

Watch your dream come alive
As YOU made it in your mind!

Be thankful again
And go back and repeat!

Miracles are awesome!

Where do YOU want to go?

What do YOU want to see?

With these steps you've now learned,
The world's at your feet!

"Do GREAT!" I'd say,
If I could to your face

And, "Share what you learned
For a world happy and safe!"

Matt Scott

AWESOME STEPS

1. Know your THOUGHTS ARE THINGS and the world can respond to them.
   AKA: BELIEVE!

2. Know you WILL achieve/receive a response to a TRUE POSITIVE thought.
   AKA: HAVE FAITH!

3. Have an OPEN HEART by continually loving your current material world unconditionally.
   AKA: FIND SOMETHING AWESOME! (Love what you see and thank the sky!)

4. Recognize and love YOU standing at the spot facing your current world with your imagination (and your past) behind you!
   AKA: FIND YOU! LOVE YOU! (THIS IS "NOW," THIS IS YOU!)

5. Picture in your now open mind/imagination/self with loving passion what YOU are seeking for your future!
   AKA: LOVE YOUR SELF!

6. BE THANKFUL (to the sky) for this miracle!
   AKA: AWARENESS (RECOGNIZE THAT ANYTHING IS POSSIBLE!)

7. Say in your head, "I am awesome, I can do this!"
   AKA: TAKE ACTION!

8. WATCH the world respond to get you there!
   AKA: SUCCEED!

9. REPEAT!
   AKA: NEVER GIVE UP! KEEP IT UP!

AWESOME CAPABILITIES

YOU can always Find Something Awesome and be Thankful to feel happy!

YOU can picture an image of what your are seeking in your brain's imagination!

YOU can recognize negativity as it comes, let it go by YOU, and reset your picture!

You can be YOU and take action and accomplish your dreams!

The cool thing is,
If you doubt what I say,

It just takes TO TRY
To PROVE it's this way!

Take a deep breath,
Smile UP at the sky!

Step 1 is all YOU!
So give it a TRY!

AWESOME QUESTIONS

1. True or False? You can always Find Something Awesome, and be thankful.

2. What does BELIEVE mean?

3. What is the opposite of DOUBT?

4. What is an open heart?

5. True or False? As presented here, your Mind, your Self, and your Imagination, are all the same thing.

6. Are YOU your Mind/Self/Imagination, or is your Mind/Self/Imagination a tool YOU can use to picture what YOU are trying to accomplish?

7. How can YOU know if your Mind/Self/Imagination is off?

8. What will negativity do to your closed Mind/Self/Imagination if you let it?

9. Are YOU the negativity you see and/or feel?

10. True or False? Thinking what others are thinking about YOU is a great way to have SELF-confidence and be creative. What is this false confidence called?

11. If you have imagined a goal, ask this: What is its PURPOSE?
AKA: "Do I want this goal so I can GET love or attention? So I can be liked?
OR, Do I want this goal because it will allow me to GIVE love? And I can help other people?
OR, It would just be plain awesome... because YOU love it... and do not 'need it' for your confidence."
If it's the first, try again!

(Love what IS, Thank the rest, Love YOU, re-imagine an awesome goal!)
DON'T GIVE AWAY YOUR LOVING PURPOSE by WANTING LOVE to be CONFIDENT!
LOVE YOU! (And now you know how to find YOU!)

12. How do YOU not let negativity affect YOU, and/or how do YOU turn a recognized bad feeling off? What stays on, and/or gets turned back on?

13. True or False? YOU stand in-between your current world that YOU see, and your image YOU created in your Mind/Self/Imagination. What is this ALSO called?

14. True or False? Obstacles can present themselves to any imagined goal.

15. True or False? An obstacle is a reason to quit.

16. Repeat after me, "I can accomplish anything I set my Mind/Self/Imagination to." True or False?

17. What is the first step?

ABOUT THE AUTHOR

"What I finally learned about true happiness as an adult, I wanted to teach kids early in life in a way that they could understand and use to get through the bumps of childhood and learn how to create their OWN happiness and success."

– Matt Scott

Matt Scott discovered the AWESOME power of our brains to find happiness and success. Now, he wants to share his discovery with all young people.

A Montana native, Matt is an active believer and dedicated reader of success and self-help books. He knows that EVERYONE'S brains are capable of creating a HAPPY and SUCCESSFUL life!

He says, **"Learning how our brains work in this world is IMPERATIVE to creating a happy and successful life!"** Matt was inspired to create the FIND SOMETHING AWESOME! book series to introduce and communicate the power of our brains in a universal way that could be understood and applied at an early age.

He wrote the series to give parents fun, yet powerful teaching tools to start the conversation, so all young people can have early knowledge of their brain's power to build self-confidence and learn how to create positive outcomes in life.

A happy childhood and successful adulthood starts with learning how to FIND SOMETHING AWESOME!

Matt loves his family, being a dad, and building friendships and community. He enjoys paddle boarding, snowboarding, and Air-Chairing! Matt lives in Los Angeles, California, with his wife and three children.

Find Something Awesome!

I AM AND I CAN!

MIND (BOX!)

A BOOK SERIES

Helping Kids Realize the Power of their Brains to Be Happy and Successful!

   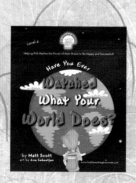 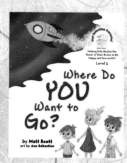

Recommended by Teachers, Therapists, Parents, & Kids!

What if you could give your children all the 'self-help' wisdom and life lessons you learned later in life in a book that they would actually love and listen to?

You can! FIND SOMETHING AWESOME! is a FUN and FRIENDLY book series that teaches kids the AWESOME power of their brains!

Kids will learn the necessary life skills to build self-confidence and create desired outcomes for Happiness and Success! This made-for-children series introduces the powers (and fun!) of Positive Thinking, Gratitude, Mindfulness, and Focused Imagination.

Building upon themselves, each book shows children what their brains are capable of doing!

Level 1: What Color Is Your Butterfly?
What we think affects how we feel! Kids will learn they can train their brain to 'FIND SOMETHING AWESOME!' to feel awesome!

Level 2: Have You Ever Thanked a Rainbow?
Gratitude leads to happiness! Helps kids understand the power (and fun!) of positive thinking and gratitude in everyday life.

Level 3: Did You Laugh When You Stubbed Your Toe?
Turn negative thinking around! Kids will learn how to recognize and turn off negative feelings, and to remain strong and confident with positive self-encouragement.

Level 4: Have You Ever Watched What Your World Does?
Positive Thinking, Gratitude, Self-encouragement, Mindfulness, and Focused Imagination lead to successful outcomes in life! Helps kids understand their brain's capabilities to help make their dreams come true!

Level 5: Where Do You Want To Go?
Imagine your dream! Kids will learn how to refuel themselves through loving their world to imagine and achieve their goals!

Do You Have a FIND SOMETHING AWESOME Story to Share?
We'd love to hear from you!

www.FindSomethingAwesome.com